The
Abandoned
Puppy

Other titles by Holly Webb

The Snow Bear

Animal Stories:

My Naughty Little Puppy:

The Abandoned Puppy

Holly Webb

Illustrated by Sophy Williams

Stripes

For Kitty

For more information about Holly Webb visit:
www.holly-webb.com

STRIPES PUBLISHING
An imprint of Little Tiger Press
1 The Coda Centre, 189 Munster Road,
London SW6 6AW

A paperback original
First published in Great Britain in 2013

Text copyright © Holly Webb, 2013
Illustrations copyright © Sophy Williams, 2013

ISBN: 978-1-84715-360-9

A CIP catalogue record for this book is available
from the British Library.

Printed and bound in the UK.

10 9 8 7 6 5 4 3 2 1

Chapter One

The littlest puppy whimpered quietly. The cardboard box had stopped bouncing up and down, but no one had come to get her out, and it was still so dark. She didn't like it. She didn't know where her mother was, and she was hungry.

She squeaked in frightened surprise as a low rumbling noise shook the box.

It seemed to be moving again, swinging and then sliding across the floor. Her two brothers slammed into her, knocking her against the side of the box as the car went round a sharp corner.

The journey seemed to go on for a very long time, but she couldn't even curl up for a sleep. Every time she managed to get comfortable, the box would slide around again, and they'd all be on top of each other. It was nothing like their rough-and-tumble puppy play in the big basket at home. This hurt, and they couldn't go and snuggle up against their mother when they wanted the game to stop.

Pressed into the furthest corner, the puppy scrabbled anxiously against her brothers. They were sitting on her again! Then she realized that they'd stopped – the box wasn't sliding around any more. Her brothers stood up cautiously. They listened, flinching a little at the creaky wheeze of the car boot opening. Then the box swung up into the air, and was dropped down with a heavy thud.

They heard footsteps, hurrying away. And then they were left alone.

"Are you ready to go, Zoe?" Auntie Jo was standing at the front door to their terraced house, wearing her wellies and her Redlands Animal Shelter fleece.

"Yes!" Zoe dashed down the hallway, stuffing the packet of dried apricots that Mum had found in the back of the cupboard into her lunchbox. She and Mum had both forgotten she'd need packed lunches this week, so Zoe's lunch was a bit random. Still, she really liked golden syrup sandwiches!

"Where's your big sister?" Auntie Jo asked, peering down the hallway into the kitchen.

"She's still asleep." Zoe shook her head. "Kyra thinks I'm mad getting up early to come with you when I don't have to."

"Well, if you stayed at home with your sister all day you'd just end up watching TV for the whole of the Easter holidays!" Mum called out. "You'll have a much better time at the shelter!"

"I heard that!" Kyra's voice floated down from upstairs. "I'm not asleep and I'm not watching TV. I'm revising! In bed! See you later, Auntie Jo. I'll come and pick Zoe up."

Kyra had her GCSEs coming up, so she was revising as hard as she could. Zoe was really glad that Auntie Jo had said she could help out at the shelter – she normally only got to help out after school. It would have been boring being stuck at home with Kyra, and Mum couldn't afford to take any time off work. Sometimes when they were off school she got to spend the day with her friend Becca, but Becca had gone to her gran's in Scotland for the fortnight.

"Thanks for letting me come for the whole day," Zoe said to Auntie Jo, as they walked to the shelter, which was about ten minutes from Zoe's house.

"That's all right!" Auntie Jo grinned at her. "I'm not going to be letting you off lightly, you know. I've got a long list of jobs for you to do, starting with cleaning out the dogs' runs, then bathing the cats, and maybe even knitting some bodywarmers for the guinea pigs..." She looked down at Zoe's worried face. "It's all right, I'm teasing you, Zo! There will be loads of useful stuff you can do, I promise, but it'll be mostly exercising the dogs, if it's not too wet. They don't get walked as much on the weekends, because that's when we get most of our visitors. They'll all be desperate for a good run around."

Redlands was quite a small shelter, but it took in every kind of animal. The staff did their best to get them all rehomed but it wasn't always easy. Auntie Jo had been working there for three years now, ever since she'd gone to the shelter to get a cat and come home with Barney, her gorgeous tabby. She had been working as a receptionist at the local vet back then. That's how she knew all about Redlands. She'd ended up volunteering to help out at the shelter in her spare time. Then, when a job had come up as manager, she'd jumped at the chance. Zoe had been delighted too.

"You're so lucky, getting to be at the shelter every day, and see all the dogs," Zoe sighed. "I'm definitely going to work somewhere like Redlands when I'm older. Or maybe I'll be a vet," she added thoughtfully.

Auntie Jo smiled at her. "It is a lovely job at the shelter," she agreed. "But it does have its sad bits too. Sometimes it makes me so angry the way people don't look after their animals properly. And it isn't always the owner's fault either. Sometimes they really love their pets, but they just can't care for them in the same way any more. That's really heartbreaking." She sighed. "I just want to take them all home with me. But four cats is quite enough."

Having just Barney the tabby hadn't lasted very long. Auntie Jo was a sucker for big fluffy cats.

"Mmmm. So, did anybody take a

dog or cat home over the weekend?"
Zoe asked. She loved hearing about the
new homes the animals went to. She
liked to imagine herself into some of
the stories Auntie Jo told. She would
have loved to have had a dog from the
shelter, but she knew they couldn't. It
wouldn't be fair to leave it all alone in
their house while Mum was at work,
and Kyra wasn't really a dog fan either.
She'd been chased across the park by a
huge Bernese Mountain Dog when she
was about four. She and Mum had
been on their way to nursery, and Kyra
had been on her scooter. The dog had
only wanted to be friendly, but Kyra
hadn't known that, and she'd fallen off
trying to get away from him. She'd
been scared of dogs ever since.

"Edward got chosen this weekend!" said Auntie Jo. "Finally! I'm so pleased, Zoe. I thought he'd never find a home!" Zoe grinned. Edward was one of the older dogs – a bulldog. A lot of people seemed to think that they were weird-looking. Everyone always wanted a cute little puppy but Edward had such a sweet nature.

"An elderly man came in," Auntie Jo went on. "He wanted Edward straightaway. He said that he'd always had bulldogs, and Edward was a smasher. That's what he called him – a little smasher!"

Zoe giggled. "I hope he isn't. He is a bit clumsy. He does bump into things."

Auntie Jo laughed. "One of the staff went round and did a home visit, because Mr Johnson was so keen to take Edward straightaway. She said it looked perfect. A nice bit of garden, and near a park for good walks. She reckoned Edward and Mr Johnson were a perfect match – both of them on the elderly side. You know Edward never liked walking very fast!"

Zoe nodded. She'd taken Edward

round the park with Auntie Jo and a couple of the other dogs from the shelter before. It was the slowest walk she'd ever been on!

"Lucky Edward. And lucky Mr Johnson," Zoe said. "I bet they're having such a lovely time." She wrapped her arm through Auntie Jo's, and leaned against her with a sigh. "I know we can't, but I do wish I could have a dog of my own..."

Chapter Two

The box seemed to be getting colder and colder. The April night had been frosty, and the puppies had huddled together to keep warm. They weren't used to being outside at night and there was only the thin cardboard box between them and the concrete steps. They had always slept in their comfortable basket, snuggled up next to their mother. The cold was a frightening shock.

The smallest of the three, the tiny girl puppy, woke up first. She was miserably stiff, the cold aching inside her, and she scrabbled worriedly at the cardboard under her paws. Her two brothers were still asleep, curled up together, but somehow during the night she had rolled away from them. Now she was on her own in the corner of the box, shivering and hungry.

She tried to scratch at the side of the box, wondering if she could get out, and somehow find her way back to her mother.

But even her claws hurt this morning, and she felt weak and sleepy. Too feeble to claw a hole in the side of a box.

She still didn't understand what had happened. Why had they been taken away from their mother, and their warm basket? Was someone going to come and get them, and take them back to her? When they'd been put into the box, she'd heard her mother barking and whining – she hadn't wanted them to go any more than they had. The littlest puppy had a horrible feeling that they might not be going back.

Zoe and her aunt were nearly at the shelter. Zoe could feel herself speeding up. She loved it when they got to be the ones who opened up at Redlands – it was a real treat, and usually only happened if Auntie Jo let her come and help on a Saturday. She knew that all the animals would be excited to see someone after the night on their own. The dogs would be the most obvious about it, jumping about and scrabbling at the wire mesh on the front of their pens, and barking like mad. But even the cats, who usually liked to be more stand-offish, would spring up from their baskets, and come to see who was there. The shelter had a big pen full of guinea pigs at the moment, so there would be mad squeaking from them as well.

Auntie Jo was searching in her bag for the keys, so it was Zoe who first noticed that there was something strange on the front steps.

"What's that?" she asked curiously, frowning at what looked like a box in front of the main door to the shelter.

Auntie Jo looked up from the bunch of keys. "What?"

"There. On the steps. Maybe someone's donated food to the shelter, Auntie Jo!" People did bring in pet food for the animals occasionally, Zoe had seen them. "It's funny that they didn't bring it in when there was someone who could say thank you, though."

"Mmmm..." Auntie Jo was walking faster now, the keys dangling forgotten in her hand.

"What's the matter?" Zoe asked. She could see that her aunt looked worried.

"People leave us other things too, Zoe," Auntie Jo sighed. "It might be an abandoned animal in that box. If it is, I suppose that at least they've brought it to us, but I hate it when they just leave it like that."

Zoe felt her eyes filling with tears. The box was just a box, a shabby cardboard one. How could someone stuff a cat or a dog in there, and then just leave it? It was so mean!

They hurried up the steps, and sat down slowly, one on either side of the lid. Auntie Jo took a deep breath. "I never get used to this," she murmured, as she started to unfold the flaps on the top. "It's been such a cold night. Look, there's frost on the top. If there's something inside, I hope it hasn't been in there long."

There was a feeble scrabbling noise from inside the box, and Zoe caught her breath. "There is something inside there!"

Auntie Jo frowned at the box. "Yes.

And I'm being silly, Zo. We should take the box inside. We don't want whoever's in here getting scared and leaping out."

Zoe nodded. "Good idea. Shall I take it?" she asked hopefully. "You unlock the door."

Carefully, Zoe slipped her hands underneath the box, shivering as she touched the clammy, cold cardboard. Whoever was in it must have spent a miserably cold night. She heaved the box up, and felt something inside it wriggle.

There was a worried little squeak, and a yap.

"It's OK," she whispered. "We're just taking you into the shelter. It'll be nice and warm in there. Well, warmer than out here, anyway."

Auntie Jo had unlocked the doors now, and she was just turning off the alarm. She held the door open for Zoe, and they hurried into the reception area, putting the box down on one of the chairs.

"I think it's a dog," Zoe told her aunt. "I definitely heard a yapping noise. But it can't be a very big dog, the box hardly weighed anything at all."

"Let's see." Auntie Jo lifted the flaps of the box — it was meant to hold packets of chocolate biscuits, Zoe noticed – and they both peered in.

Staring anxiously up at them were three tiny brown-and-white puppies.

Chapter Three

The littlest puppy flinched back against the side of the box. She was still so tired from being bounced and shaken around, and now the light was flooding in, after hours of being shut in the dark. It hurt her eyes and she whimpered unhappily. Her bigger, stronger brothers recovered more quickly, bouncing up to see what was happening, and where they were. But the little girl puppy pressed her nose into the corner of the box, hiding away from the light. She was too cold and tired to get up, anyway.

Zoe and her aunt gazed inside, and Zoe pushed her hand into Auntie Jo's. She'd never seen such little puppies at the shelter, she was sure. They were the smallest pups she'd ever seen anywhere. "Oh my goodness, three of them," murmured Auntie Jo.

"They're so tiny," Zoe whispered. "They can hardly weigh anything at all."

Auntie Jo nodded. "Mmmm. They're far too young to be away from their mother, really. They can only be a few weeks old. Well done for keeping quiet, Zo. We don't want to scare them.

They may not be used to seeing different people."

The puppies were looking up at Zoe and Auntie Jo uncertainly. One of the boy puppies scrabbled hopefully at the side of the box, clearly wanting to be lifted out.

"Well, he's not shy," Auntie Jo laughed quietly.

Very gently, she slipped her hands into the box, and lifted out the puppy.  He wagged his stubby little tail, and licked her fingers. "Yes, you're a darling, aren't you?" She turned to Zoe.

"They must be starving if they've been in this box all night. Now I can see him properly, I don't think this little boy can be more than four weeks old. He's probably only just been weaned from his mother. They should be having four or five meals a day, and a bit of their mum's milk still."

Zoe giggled. "That's why he's trying to eat your fingers..." Then she looked worriedly down into the box. "Auntie Jo, what about the little puppy in the corner? Is she OK? She isn't moving like the other two."

Her aunt sighed. "No, she isn't... We'd better have a look at her. Can you bring the box along to one of the puppy pens? Then we'll have somewhere cosy for them to curl up, and we can mix up some puppy milk. Maybe a little bit of Weetabix mixed in it too. We'll have to see what they think. They may not have had any solid food yet."

Zoe gently lifted up the box, with two puppies still in it, and followed her aunt through to the main shelter area, where all the pens were. Dogs jumped up excitedly as they came past, barking for their breakfast, and for someone to come and make a fuss of them. Zoe looked down worriedly at the two puppies in the box. The bigger one – she was pretty sure it was another boy – was now standing up, balancing carefully on plump little paws, and listening to the new and exciting noises. He looked up curiously at Zoe – the only person he could see at the moment.

Maybe he thinks it's me barking! Zoe thought to herself, smiling down at him.

But her smile faded as she looked over to his litter-mate. The tiny puppy was still curled miserably in the corner of the box. She didn't seem to want to get up and see what was going on at all.

"We'll put them in here – nice and close to the kitchen," Auntie Jo said, opening one of the pen doors, and crooning to the puppy snuggled in the crook of her arm. "I'm pretty sure we've got a big tin of that powdered puppy milk replacement left," Auntie Jo murmured. "And some of the made-up bottles. I'd better order some more though."

She sat down on the floor in the pen

with the puppy in her arms, and Zoe put the box down next to her, kneeling beside it. "Should we take the others out?" she asked, looking at the boy puppy, who was clawing excitedly at the side of the box now.

Auntie Jo nodded. "Be careful though, Zoe. Don't scare them. They might not be very big, but puppies can still nip if they're frightened. Get the bigger puppy out first, then we can let him explore with this one, while we see what's the matter with the tiny one."

Zoe reached in and picked up the puppy, who was still standing up against the side of the box. He wriggled and yapped excitedly and when she put him down on her lap, he squirmed around eagerly, trying to see everything in the pen. Then he nuzzled Zoe's fingers, and wriggled carefully down the leg of her jeans, making for the floor. He obviously just wanted to go exploring this new place.

The other boy puppy was still snuggled on Auntie Jo's lap, looking around curiously, but not quite confident enough to go marching around like his brother.

"Try just giving the little one a gentle stroke," Auntie Jo advised. "Don't go straight in and pick her up. She isn't looking at us, and she'd get a shock."

Zoe reached in and ran one finger down the puppy's silky back. The brown fur was so soft, but she didn't feel as warm as her brother. "She's pretty cold," Zoe said, glancing round at Auntie Jo. "Even just touching her. And she's sort of floppy."

Auntie Jo bit her lip. "She's suffered more being out all night because she's smaller. Here, put this on your lap, Zoe." She lifted a soft fleece blanket out of a padded basket in the corner of the pen. "Then lift her out carefully, and wrap her up. Just loosely. And keep your hands round her to warm her up a bit."

Zoe nodded, and gently cupped one hand around the puppy. The tiny dog shivered a little as she felt Zoe's fingers, and turned her head slightly. But she was just too weak to look up. Zoe slipped the other hand underneath her, and lifted her out on to the blanket. She swathed it round the puppy, stroking her gently through the folds.

"OK, little one," Auntie Jo murmured to the puppy on her lap. "I need to go and get your sister a hot-water bottle. And make up some milk for you guys. Hmm? Want to go and see this nice basket?" She lifted the puppy in, and stroked him for a few seconds until he got used to being somewhere new. Then she got up slowly. The other boy puppy trotted over to the basket too, nosing affectionately at his brother.

"Those two seem fine," she said, sounding relieved. "And I'm sure they'll be even perkier once they've had something to eat."

Zoe looked up at her. "What about this one?" Her voice wobbled. "You don't think she's going to be all right?"

Auntie Jo sighed. "We don't know yet. She seems very weak. I'm going to call Sam at the vet's and ask if she'll come over as soon as she can and have a look at them all. Are you OK with them for a minute, while I get a hot water bottle for the little one?"

Zoe nodded, still gently rubbing the puppy through the blanket. She wished she could feel her moving. The puppy felt like a saggy little bean bag, slumped on her lap. Carefully she moved the blanket from round the puppy's head, peering down at her. Her eyes were closed, and her pink tongue was slightly sticking out of her mouth. It looked dry, Zoe thought worriedly. Auntie Jo had better hurry up with that puppy milk. She hoped they'd be able to persuade the pup to drink it. She didn't look like she wanted to make the effort to do anything just at the minute.

"Here's the hot water bottle," Auntie Jo said, hurrying back. "I've wrapped it up so it isn't too hot."

"Do we lie her on top of it?" Zoe asked, starting to lift the puppy off her lap.

"No, that would be too hot. I'm going to put it at the side of the basket, then she can snuggle next to it. We'll just have to keep an eye on her brothers, and make sure they don't nudge her away."

"Maybe we ought to put her in a pen on her own," Zoe said doubtfully. "They're a lot bigger than she is. They might push her around."

"I'd rather keep them together if we

can. She's already lost her mother, and her home. Her brothers are the only security she knows. Also, if we separate her, she might find it difficult to manage being around other dogs when she's bigger."

Zoe nodded as she laid the puppy close to the hot water bottle. "We don't want her to be lonely," she agreed.

"I've started to warm up some puppy milk. I'll just go and get it, and we can see what they think." Auntie Jo nipped into the kitchen, and came back with a shallow metal tray of the special puppy milk. "Hopefully they won't tip this over," she explained to Zoe, who was looking at the tray in surprise – it looked like something her mum would make chocolate brownies in.

The two boy puppies had been nosing around the edges of the pen, trying to explore, but as soon as Auntie Jo put the tray down, they galloped over to see what it was – so fast that they got tangled up, and fell over each other. They struggled to their feet, mock-growling, and then scurried up to the tray, sniffing at it excitedly. It only took seconds before they were eagerly lapping, burying their tiny muzzles in the milk and splashing it around.

"They must have had milk from bowls before," Zoe said, watching them and giggling.

"Maybe. Or else they're just fast learners," said Auntie Jo. "I don't think we need to worry about them not feeding. I'll mix a bit of Weetabix into the next lot." But she was frowning. "I'd really hoped that the smell would wake the little one up, but she doesn't seem to have noticed. We'll have to try feeding it to her by the bottle."

Zoe nodded. "Shall I put her on my lap?" she asked hopefully. She'd loved holding the puppy before, and trying to warm her up. Even though it was frightening that the puppy was ill, it felt really special to be the ones trying to make her better.

"Yes. Unwrap her, and we'll try to get her to take a bottle. I brought one just in case." Auntie Jo took a baby's bottle with a cap out of the pocket of her fleece, and sat down next to Zoe. "She's still so sleepy…"

The puppy was really floppy now, and she didn't wriggle when Zoe unwrapped her. Auntie Jo held the teat of the bottle up to her mouth, but she didn't seem to notice it. She certainly didn't start sucking, as Zoe had hoped she would. She only turned her head away a little, as though Auntie Jo nudging the bottle against her mouth was annoying.

"She doesn't want it," Zoe said worriedly. "Is there anything else we can give her?"

"We could try using a syringe..." Auntie Jo said thoughtfully. "We can poke it into the corner of her mouth, and try and trickle it in." But Zoe could see that her aunt was doubtful about the puppy ever feeding at all.

"What about..." Zoe brushed her fingers against the teat, letting a few drops of milk ooze out of the tiny hole on to her fingers. It was thick and yellowish, not like ordinary milk at all. Holding her breath, she stroked her milky fingers across the puppy's mouth, letting the milk run on to the dry, pink tongue.

The puppy shivered with surprise, and the little tongue darted out, licking Zoe's fingers.

"She likes it!" Zoe squeaked.

Auntie Jo smiled. "Quick, you take the bottle. Squeeze a little out on to the end of the teat, and dribble it into her mouth."

The puppy licked eagerly at the teat this time, and when Zoe pushed it gently against her mouth, she sucked, harder and harder, until she was slurping messily at the milk.

And then, at last, she opened her dark eyes, and stared up at Zoe.

Chapter Four

To: Becca
From: Zoe
Subject: Puppies

Hi Becca!

Hope you're having a good time at your gran's. Sorry I've not mailed you for a couple of days. Been sooooo busy! I went to the shelter with Auntie Jo on Monday, and someone had abandoned three puppies in a box on the front steps!!! (Here's a photo.

Auntie Jo took it on her phone. Aren't they gorgeous?) It was a box that was meant to be for chocolate biscuits, so we've called the two boys Choc and Biscuit, and the little girl puppy Cookie. She's really lovely. When we first found them she was really weak and Auntie Jo told me afterwards she wasn't sure she was going to make it. We're giving her milk from a bottle because she won't eat mashed-up Weetabix, even though her two brothers love it! (You should see them eating, it goes everywhere, we have to wash them afterwards!) But some of it must be going inside them - they're getting fatter every day! Cookie is definitely getting bigger too, and she likes me to carry her round everywhere! I've got lots more photos that Mum's printed out for me, I'll show you when you get back.

Love Zoe xxxxxxxxxxxxx

I can't believe you found puppies! You are so lucky. Gran's is OK but it's a bit cold as it's by the sea. I went paddling and my toes almost fell off.

Will the puppies get new owners from the shelter? How old are they? I wish I could come and see them. Guess what? Mum and Dad say we can definitely have a dog (you know they wouldn't make up their minds before). But now they say we have to go slow and make sure we find the right dog! Aaargh! I really want to have a dog NOW! When I get back please ask your auntie if I can come and see the puppies. Maybe one of them could be our dog!!!

From Becca xxxxxxxxxxx

Zoe read Becca's reply to her email, smiling to herself. Becca wrote emails just like she talked. But her smile faded a little as she read on to the end. Becca was so lucky to be allowed a dog. Zoe had been talking to Auntie Jo about the puppies today at the shelter. They'd been weighing them to check that they were eating enough, which was quite difficult because Choc, Biscuit and Cookie saw no reason why they should stand still on top of the scales, and just kept bouncing around. In the end, Auntie Jo had made a guess at their weights, but she said they were definitely getting heavier, which was the main thing.

Then they'd taken five minutes just to play with the puppies – it seemed like fun, rather than work, but Zoe knew it was actually really important. If the puppies didn't ever get played with, they wouldn't know how to behave with their new owners.

"How could anyone have abandoned them?" Zoe said sadly, watching Biscuit and Choc bombing up and down the pen, chasing after a ball. Cookie was scampering after them, not quite brave enough or fast enough to take the ball off her brothers, but having just as much fun. "They're so gorgeous, all of them. How could anyone be so mean?"

Auntie Jo sighed. "Well, at least they brought them here. It was a start."

"But they left them out in the cold all night!"

"Mmm. Some people just don't think. The puppies were probably an accident – they hadn't had the mum spayed, and then maybe the owners felt they couldn't afford to buy all the puppy food, and take the puppies to the vet for vaccinations. Dogs are expensive to look after." She reached over to put her arm round Zoe's shoulders. "Don't think about it, Zo. The puppies were lucky they ended up here, so they've got all of us looking after them. We're going to turn them into lovely, well-behaved dogs, and make sure they only go to fab owners. They won't remember their horrible start."

"I hope not," Zoe whispered, with a tiny sigh. Auntie Jo's words were meant to make her feel better. She knew the puppies would need to leave the shelter in a few weeks, but she'd been trying not to think about it too much. She'd only known them for a few days, but they were so sweet, Cookie especially. If they could stay at the shelter for a bit longer, she'd be able to keep on looking after them… But that wasn't fair. They needed proper homes.

Reading the exciting news in Becca's email had made her think about having to say goodbye to the puppies all over again…

To: Becca
From: Zoe
Subject: Puppies

Hi Becca

Auntie Jo thinks the puppies were about four weeks old when we found them, so now they're five weeks. They can't go to new homes until they're about eight weeks old. I'm sure you can come and see them, I'll ask Auntie Jo. You're so lucky getting a dog!

I hope your mum and dad decide on one
soon. See you back at school in a week!
Love Zoe xx

It wasn't as friendly as her emails to
Becca usually were, but Zoe was feeling
sad. She stared at her computer screen,
not really seeing the cute photo of
Cookie that she had set as her
wallpaper.

"What's up?"

Zoe jumped. She hadn't heard Mum come in at all. "Nothing... I was just thinking about the puppies. I'm going to miss them so much when they get rehomed." She gulped. "Especially Cookie."

Mum nodded. "She is gorgeous." Zoe had shown Mum the puppies one afternoon at the shelter, when Mum had come to pick her up. "I think it's her eyes. She's got such a little face, it makes her eyes look huge, and then she's got those lovely whiskery eyebrows. Has Auntie Jo worked out what breed they are yet?"

Zoe giggled and shook her head. "Nope. Everyone at Redlands thinks they're something different. Auntie Jo reckons maybe there's some Jack Russell in them and maybe some Cockapoo too. But we might not be able to tell until they're bigger. Almost grown-up. And we won't have them then, will we? So we'll never know." She sniffed, and Mum hugged her.

"But you knew they'd have to go to new homes, Zo! All the animals at the shelter do. You've never got this upset before."

"I know. Maybe it was because we found them – and feeding Cookie with the bottle has made her special to me, Mum." Zoe smiled proudly. "I got her to take some puppy mix and milk in a bowl this morning. Auntie Jo was really pleased, she said that she'd thought Cookie was going to have to be on bottles for ever!"

"Your Auntie Jo ought to be paying you wages!" Mum sighed. "I know you love it at the shelter, but maybe you should have a couple of days off from helping out? Do something else? I bet Kyra could take enough time away from her revision to take you shopping. Or the cinema?"

Zoe looked horrified. "Oh no, Mum! I've got to keep going. I've got to help Cookie get on with the solid food. It's really important."

Her mum gave her a worried look. "Well, I suppose so…"

Chapter Five

"It sounds like the best Easter holidays ever!" Becca sighed enviously.

Zoe smiled at her as they walked into their classroom. "It was fab. I really missed going to the shelter this morning. I was looking forward to seeing you, but apart from that I could have done without school!"

"Me too, but I can't see my mum

letting me have the day off because I needed to go and visit the world's cutest puppies…" Becca flopped down into her chair, and glanced over at the board. "Numeracy problems! Great start to the new term…" She got out her maths book, but went on talking in a whisper. "So is Cookie properly weaned now? She's eating real puppy food?"

Zoe nodded. "Yup, they all still have a bit of milk, but they've started drinking water too. And Cookie's really catching up with Biscuit and Choc. I don't think she'll ever be quite as big as they are, but she's doing OK. I brought the photos Mum printed out – I'll show you at break— Ssh! – Mrs Allan's watching us right now." She stopped talking and tried to look like she was concentrating on the problems that Mrs Allan had put on the board for them. Their teacher was usually lovely, but she always got extra strict when they came back after the holidays – as though she thought they needed to remember what school was like!

Zoe showed the photos to Becca and some of the other girls in her class at break time, and everyone said how gorgeous the puppies were. Lots of the girls said they were going to ask their mums and dads if they could come to the shelter and see the puppies, and maybe even adopt one of them. Zoe knew that most of her friends wouldn't be allowed to – Lucy already had two dogs at home, for a start! But the more people who came to see the puppies the better. However much Zoe hated the thought of them leaving the shelter, she wanted them to have the very best of homes.

That afternoon, Auntie Jo had arranged to nip out from the shelter and pick Zoe up from school. Mum was going to fetch her after she finished work. Zoe got changed quickly in the staff loos – Mum hated her getting her school uniform messy – and then ran to see Cookie and the others.

Cookie was curled up in their basket, watching her brothers playing tug-of-war with a bit of old rope that someone had given them. They'd had it since the morning, and it was their new favourite toy. Bits of it were scattered all over the pen. She sighed a little, and rested her nose on her paws, wondering where Zoe was. Zoe had played with her every day since they'd come here from their old home. Actually, the little puppy couldn't remember much of where they'd lived before they'd been at the shelter. The only thing she was sure of was that their mother had been at the old place. She still wondered what had happened, and why they had been

63

taken away, but she didn't mind, because now she had Zoe.

Except that today she didn't, and she didn't understand why. Zoe always fed her and her brothers. Zoe made a special fuss of them, even though she wasn't feeding milk from her lap any more. Zoe still brought the food bowls, and watched to make sure that she was eating properly. Zoe even stopped Choc and Biscuit from trying to take her food if they finished theirs first.

Today the other lady had brought their food - Jo, the one who was always with Zoe. Jo had said nice things, and she'd stroked her, and said how good she was. But it wasn't the same.

Cookie's little ears pricked up sharply. Someone was running along the passage

between the pens - someone with small, light footsteps. She jumped up in the basket and barked excitedly as Zoe appeared at the front of the pen, beaming at her.

"Oh! Did you miss me? I really missed you," Zoe told her, opening the latch. "You too, yes, I missed you as well, you great big monsters," she told Biscuit and Choc, patting them lovingly as they waltzed round her feet. But it was Cookie that she sat down next to, and Cookie she cuddled as soon as the puppy clambered happily into her lap.

"I missed you more," Zoe whispered into her ears, as she stroked her. "I know I shouldn't really say it, but I did." She sighed. "There's some people come to look round, Cookie. Try and look like a perfect pet, won't you? You aren't old enough to go for a couple more weeks, but if they like you, they might wait."

She could hear them coming along the line of pens, now. A couple, who'd just bought a house together, and were thinking of getting a dog. They'd said they didn't mind whether it was a puppy or an older dog, but when Auntie Jo had mentioned the three gorgeous little puppies they had got excited.

"They'll be looking out for you." Zoe sighed again. "They looked nice,

I suppose. Nice-ish…" She couldn't imagine anyone being a good enough owner for her lovely Cookie. No one except her, she realized, with a miserable little gulp.

"So they decided on Jasper?" Zoe asked as she helped her aunt to clean out the food bowls, feeling a bit surprised, but very relieved. Jasper was about five years old and was a mixed-breed, mostly Labrador. He wasn't nearly as nice-looking as Cookie and her brothers, Zoe thought.

"Yes, they decided that they wanted a bigger dog after all," Auntie Jo explained. "Don't worry, Zoe. It won't be hard to find homes for those three at all. They're gorgeous. It's the older dogs that it can be hard to place."

Zoe nodded. "My friend Becca is going to get a dog soon. Becca said she'd love to come and see the puppies. She's going to ask her mum and dad if they could come this weekend. That would be OK, wouldn't it?" Her voice wobbled a little bit. "It'll only be one more week till the puppies are old enough to go to new homes then…"

Auntie Jo looked closely at her. "Yes, they'll be about seven weeks this weekend, as far as we can tell. It won't hurt them to be split up from their litter after eight weeks. It would be lovely for one of your friends to come. Zoe, are you OK, sweetheart?"

"I'll miss them, that's all," Zoe muttered.

"I know you will. Especially Cookie. You've looked after her so well. But she can't stay here, Zo, you know that. It isn't a good life for a dog, in a little pen like this, however much we love them."

"I know. But it's hard to think of someone else taking her home. I wish we could have a dog! I'd look after her so well!" Zoe burst out. Then she added quietly, "Don't worry, I know we can't..."

Auntie Jo hugged her, accidentally clanging two stainless steel dishes together behind her back, and making Zoe laugh.

"I'm so excited!" Becca raced up the steps towards Zoe, her mum following behind. She flung her arms round her. "Please can we see *all* the dogs? And the cats? I know we don't want a cat, but I'd like to see them anyway. And the guinea pigs!"

"I'll show you everything," Zoe promised, giggling. She hadn't seen her friend so hyper since her birthday party. She took them all round the shelter, saving the dog pens until last.

"You're so lucky, getting to help here all the time," Becca told her, cooing at the guinea pigs. Then she looked excitedly up at her mum. "Please can you show us the dogs now, Zoe? Mum and Dad said we might be able to get one really soon. That's what Dad's doing today – mending our garden fence so that there aren't any holes round the bottom of it, and it's safe for a dog to be in the garden. He said if we found a dog from somewhere like here, the shelter would want to come and check that we'd look after it properly."

Zoe nodded. "Yes, Auntie Jo and the other staff go and look around everyone's houses. They wouldn't let you have a cat from here if you lived on a really busy road. Or if you had small children. You'll be all right," she added. "You want a dog and it's only *really* small children that are a problem – you know, too small to understand about not pulling tails."

Becca nodded.

"Doesn't your dad want to help choose a dog?" Zoe asked curiously.

Becca's mum smiled. "This is just a first look – so we can think about what sort of dog we'd like. Becca's dad will come and see them if we tell him there's a dog we really like the look of. But he started worrying about the fence last night, and he was determined to get it done. He didn't want us to miss out on a lovely dog because the house wasn't ready."

Zoe smiled. It sounded as though Becca and her mum and dad were really serious about getting a dog. They weren't just deciding to adopt one without thinking it through, like some people did. "OK, look, well here are the dog pens. It can get a bit noisy!" she warned Becca, as several of the dogs started to bark excitedly when they realized they had visitors.

"Oh, look..." Becca whispered, glancing from side to side. "So many!

Freddie… Luca – he's gorgeous, Mum, look! He looks like a German Shepherd. Oooh! Trixie!" Becca crouched down by the little spaniel's pen. "She's so pretty…"

She glanced up worriedly at Zoe. "How do people ever choose? She's looking at me, like she really wants us to take her home, and I haven't even gone halfway along the pens yet!"

"It is hard," Zoe admitted. "If you think you really like any of the dogs, tell me, and I'll ask Auntie Jo if you can go into the pen and meet them."

"If I did that I'd never be able to say no," Becca's mum muttered. "What if we cuddled a dog and then said we didn't want him? It would be heartbreaking!"

Zoe wrinkled her nose. She supposed she was more used to the shelter than most people. "I know it's sad. But Auntie Jo and the others do find homes for all the dogs in the end. It does take a while for some of them, though." She led Becca and her mum along the row of pens. "And these..." she stopped by a pen, "are the puppies

75

we found abandoned." She laughed as all three of them raced towards the wire of the pen. "The one with the darker brown patches is Choc and that one's Biscuit..." She pointed to the puppy with the brown eyepatch. "And this one, with the pale brown patches," she paused, "is Cookie."

"Oh, wow..." Becca murmured. "They're all so beautiful!"

"They are lovely," her mum agreed. "They look very little, Zoe. Are they old enough to be rehomed?"

"Not for about another week," Zoe explained. "But then it will be fine, although they still can't go outside for a while after that. All the dogs in here have been vaccinated, but puppies have to have a last lot of vaccinations when they're about twelve weeks old. Then they can go for walks. They'd be OK in the garden though," she added.

"You know loads about dogs," Becca said admiringly. "Please can we meet them properly? Mum, do you want to?"

Her mum nodded, smiling. "Definitely."

Zoe swallowed hard, and opened the catch on the pen. It was a good thing that Becca and her mum liked the puppies. But it was one step closer to them leaving the shelter, and Zoe.

Cookie scrabbled excitedly at the wire. Zoe had been playing with them that morning, and then she'd disappeared. Now she was back!

But there were other people too. Another girl, like Zoe, and someone else. Cookie had never seen them before. She stopped wagging her tail quite so hard, and backed up a bit as Zoe opened the door. She wasn't used to different people.

Zoe let Becca and her mum in, and Biscuit and Choc sniffed cautiously at them. Becca picked up the last bit of the rope toy, and whisked it along the ground, right in front of Choc, who quickly pounced on it, pretending to growl.

"He's so funny!" Becca giggled.

"I think he's the friendliest of the pups," Zoe told her. She looked round for Cookie, who was almost hiding behind her, watching Becca and her mum with big, anxious eyes. "It's all right, Cookie," she whispered.

Cookie pressed herself against Zoe's side, and sniffed cautiously at Becca's mum's fingers when she held them out. The new people smelled nice, but she didn't know them like she knew Zoe. She didn't mind if this lady stroked her though.

"She's very sweet," Becca's mum said. "Is this the one you bottle-fed, Zoe? You can see that she adores you."

Zoe smiled sadly. She loved it that Cookie acted like her dog, even though she wasn't. She sighed. Cookie was going to have to learn to love somebody else. Gently, she lifted Cookie up, and put her on Becca's mum's lap.

Cookie froze, and sat motionless, her shoulders all hunched up under her ears. She looked round at Zoe worriedly, but she didn't wriggle off. It was all right. Zoe was still there, very close. The lady stroked her ears, which was nice. She relaxed a little, and licked her hand.

"She's a tiny bit shy, but she's very loving," Zoe said, trying not to mind someone else cuddling Cookie. She took a deep breath. "She'd be a brilliant pet. Any of them would."

Cookie watched sadly, her ears flattening back, as they all got up. They were going, she could tell. She missed Zoe so much now that she didn't stay all day the way she used to. Zoe had been here for longer today, but Cookie still hadn't had her tea. Cookie liked it when Zoe brought her food, and sat with her while she ate. She always ate more when Zoe was there, because Zoe liked to see her eat, and she would tell her what a good dog she was, eating so nicely.

As Zoe was shutting the front of the pen, Cookie raced after her, scrabbling her claws against the wire netting and whining sadly.

"It's OK," Zoe whispered to her. "I'll be back tomorrow. I promise."

Cookie didn't know what that meant, but she understood Zoe's comforting voice. She stopped whining, and just stood up against the wire, staring after the girls as they walked down the passageway between the pens. She watched until the doors swung shut, and she couldn't see Zoe any more. Then she dropped down, and sadly padded over to their basket, her claws clicking against the worn lino on the floor.

Chapter Six

"Mum says we can make pancakes for after tea," Becca told Zoe happily, as they took their coats off.

"I love pancakes," Zoe said, trying to sound a bit more cheerful than she felt. It was a treat to go to Becca's house, but she would have preferred to have stayed at the shelter with Cookie and the others for a bit longer. It would be rude to say that, though.

The girls curled up on the sofa and watched a film. Zoe was careful not to let herself think about how nice it would be if there were a little puppy snuggled up between them watching as well. But then, next time there might be. Becca's dad was still outside fixing the fence. When they'd got back, he'd shown them the shiny new wire neatly running round the base of the old wooden fence. They'd taken him out a cup of tea, and a plate of biscuits, and he'd said gratefully that he thought he was nearly finished. It looked like their whole family was really committed to having a dog.

Becca had gone to get them both some juice, leaving Zoe watching the film – they'd both seen it before – and now she came running back in.

"Zoe! I've just been talking to Mum and Dad, and guess what!"

Zoe blinked at her in surprise.

"We're going to ask your aunt if we can reserve one of the three puppies! Mum's ringing her now! She's arranging for them to come and do a home visit too!" Becca was dancing round the room in delight, and Zoe stared at her.

This was good news. One of the puppies was going to have a brilliant home, and be beautifully looked after. Zoe would even be able to keep on seeing whichever puppy they chose. She'd know what the puppies would look like when they were grown up, after all!

But what if they chose Cookie? the voice inside Zoe's head niggled. Then Cookie would belong to someone else. She stopped herself. This was her best friend, Becca, they were talking about. Cookie would have a brilliant home.

"That's wonderful," she told Becca finally, swallowing back the lump in her throat. "Auntie Jo will be really pleased."

"Oh, and Mum says tea's ready," Becca added.

Zoe nodded. That was good. After tea it would be time for her to go home, and she wouldn't have to go on trying to be happy for Becca. She knew that she ought to be, but she wasn't.

She was burningly, horribly jealous instead, and she felt terrible for it.

"We went out yesterday to that big pet shop over by the supermarket. Have you ever been there?"

Zoe shook her head.

"I hadn't either. It's enormous, and it sells everything! You'd love it, Zoe," Becca burbled happily. "Your auntie emailed Mum a long list of stuff we'll need, and we even got some things that weren't on the list, just because they were so lovely! Lots of toys! The puppies loved playing with those toys they had in their pen at the shelter, didn't they?"

Zoe nodded. "Yes," she murmured quietly, burying her head as she got her pencilcase and book out of her bag.

"And we have to make sure that our puppy has lots to do, because they might be lonely without any others to play with. Although I'll be there, of course. Zoe, are you OK?" Becca added. "You're ever so quiet."

"I'm fine." Zoe tried to sound enthusiastic. "Did you get a rope toy? They really like that old bit of rope they've got."

"Yes! A beautiful one. Much nicer than that ratty old bit they have now."

Zoe sniffed, trying not to cry. *But they like that ratty old bit of rope,* she thought to herself. *And what if Becca chooses Cookie?* Zoe stopped herself. Whichever puppy Becca chose was going to be so lucky.

I'd be a good owner too, she said to herself miserably. *I know so much about looking after dogs. I've fed those puppies, and cleaned up after them, and washed them when they got themselves covered in Weetabix...*

"Did you hear me, Zoe?" Becca nudged her gently, and Zoe jumped.

"Um, no. Sorry. What?"

"I just said that we're going to come to the shelter on Saturday, and choose the puppy, and then it can come home with us!"

"Oh!" So soon! Zoe swallowed hard. "That's great," she muttered. "Um, I really need the loo. Tell Mrs Allan, if she comes, OK?"

Zoe tried as hard as she could to be her usual self with Becca that week, but it was so, so difficult.

Becca clearly knew that something was wrong – she wasn't stupid. Zoe kept avoiding her, and nipping off to change her library book instead of chatting with Becca and their other friends at lunch time. She spent the whole of one morning break hiding in the girls' loos, after Becca started telling her about the gorgeous collars she'd seen on a pet website. They had little pawprint designs woven in to them, and space for a phone number, so that if the dog got lost it was easy for someone to call you. It had just made Zoe feel too upset. She'd had to tell Becca she felt sick when the bell went.

Zoe hated lying to her friend all of the time, but she didn't want to admit how jealous and nasty she was really feeling.

By Friday, Becca had stopped telling her about all the things they were doing to get ready for the puppy. She almost wasn't talking to Zoe at all. And at lunch she went off and played Chain-It with a group of other girls in their class, without even asking Zoe if she wanted to join in.

"See you tomorrow morning then," she told Zoe, rather awkwardly, as they got their coats on at the end of the day.

Zoe nodded. "Yes. Bye, Becca."

And that was that. No running out to the gate together. No promises to call later about homework. Becca just walked away, leaving Zoe fiddling with the zip on her jacket, and feeling totally miserable.

Kyra was waiting for her outside school as usual – the secondary school was just up the road from Zoe's, and she usually got out later than Zoe did, but Zoe had taken ages that afternoon.

"Are you all right?" she asked. "You look really down."

Zoe shrugged. "I'm sort of not talking to Becca," she admitted. "It's horrible."

"Did you have a fight?" her sister

asked sympathetically.

"No." Zoe sighed. "It's all my fault. You know the puppies at the shelter?"

Kyra laughed. "No, Zoe, it's not as if you've ever talked about them at home."

Zoe swung her schoolbag at her sister, making a face. But Kyra was always good at cheering her up. "She's going to adopt one."

Kyra smiled, and then looked confused. "But that's good, isn't it?"

"Yes," Zoe said, in a small voice. "I just wish I could too, that's all. I'm jealous… And worse than that, I'm worried that she might choose Cookie."

"Oh, Zo…" Kyra hugged her. "Look, I haven't met these puppies but I can see how much they mean to you. Why don't we stop off at the shelter, so you can show me them?"

"But you hate dogs!" Zoe stared at her.

"I don't hate them." Kyra shrugged. "I think I'm getting better. One of my friends at school has got a really cute spaniel. I even let him sit on my lap on the sofa the other day."

"Wow, Kyra! That's great!" Zoe smiled. "Of course I'll show you the puppies. You're going to love them, 'specially Cookie – she's gorgeous. I was going to ask Mum if she could take me over there later, but let's go now." She grabbed Kyra's hand, and practically towed her down the road.

"All right, all right, keep your hair on!" Kyra grinned.

It didn't take them long to walk across

the park towards Redlands and soon they were turning into the driveway.

"I've brought Kyra to see the puppies!" she told Auntie Jo, as they popped their heads round the office door.

Auntie Jo looked up from her computer. "Hi Kyra!" She grinned. "That's great news."

"Hi Auntie Jo." Kyra smiled back. "I just thought I'd like to see them. Mum said they were really cute."

"They are." Auntie Jo nodded. "I'll call your mum and tell her you're both here. I can run you home in the car if you like."

"That would be great," said Zoe. "Come on, Kyra – they're down here." Zoe grabbed Kyra's hand and pulled her down the corridor. "Don't worry.

I don't think there are any really big dogs in the shelter at the moment," she added, seeing her sister glancing cautiously into the pens.

"I just don't like it when they jump against the wire," Kyra murmured.

"Biscuit and Choc do jump up, but they're really little," Zoe promised. "Cookie won't, not till she's worked out who you are, she's a bit shy."

"OK. Oh, Zoe, are these them?" Kyra stopped in front of the puppies' pen, smiling at them delightedly. They were all asleep, for once, flopped in a sort of puppy pile in their basket. The pile heaved and wriggled every so often, and as Zoe gently undid the front of the pen, it struggled apart and turned into three hairy, whiskery brown-and-white puppies who frisked happily around Zoe's feet.

"Do you want me to bring one of the puppies out?" Zoe asked. "Then you could stroke just one – you wouldn't have them jumping about."

Kyra nodded, and Zoe picked Cookie up. Cookie nuzzled at her happily. She'd been hoping that Zoe would come soon. She looked around curiously as Zoe carried her out of the pen, leaving her two brothers behind, looking rather jealous. Cookie stared down at them, wagging her stubby little tail.

Zoe was carrying her to another girl, a taller girl with the same dark hair and eyes. Cookie looked at her with her head on one side – she looked very like Zoe. But she didn't seem to be confident with dogs the way that Zoe was. She was looking rather nervous and, as she put out her hand, she patted her very quickly, as if she thought Cookie might snap.

Curious about this girl who looked so much like her favourite person, Cookie wriggled in Zoe's arms, stretching towards the other girl.

"She likes you!" Zoe said laughing.

"Does she?" Kyra asked, sounding surprised, and rather pleased.

"Yes, she does," said Zoe. "Do you want to hold her?"

"I don't know..." Kyra looked uncertain. "OK, let me try." Kyra nodded slowly, then let Zoe put Cookie into her arms.

Cookie snuggled up against Kyra's chin, and slowly, Kyra petted her ears. The little dog closed her eyes.

"Oh, Zoe, she's gorgeous." Kyra smiled down at the puppy. "No wonder you've been spending so much time here."

"She is, isn't she?" Zoe sighed sadly. "And now I just can't bear to think of letting her go…"

Chapter Seven

Cookie scampered down the outdoor yard, chasing after the jingly ball. It was her favourite toy. She loved the noise it made, even though she didn't quite understand where the noise came from. It was definitely hers – Zoe had given it to her. It was the only toy she bothered to fight over.

Biscuit raced past her and dived on to

the ball, rolling over with it with his paws, and growling excitedly.

Cookie let out a sharp, furious bark, and jumped on top of him, scrabbling to get the ball back. Unfortunately, Biscuit was still quite a bit bigger than she was, and he wriggled and growled. Then somehow he was sitting on top of her instead, and he still had the ball, in his teeth now. He shook it backwards and forwards, still growling, so that it jingled madly.

"Stop squabbling, you two!" Zoe ran over. "Biscuit, Biscuit, look! Stretchy bone! Your best bone! Come on! Where's it going?"

Biscuit sprang up, dropping the ball, and dancing round in circles as Zoe waved the blue rubber bone. Then she flung it down the yard, and he galloped after it like a racehorse.

Cookie seized her ball gratefully, and sat down on Zoe's feet, panting.

"You really love that, don't you?" Zoe reached down and picked her up. "Look, there's a nice sunny patch there. Let's just sit and watch those two brothers of yours being mad..."

It was a beautiful warm May day, and Zoe had shorts on for the first time that year. She ought to have been feeling happy, but all she could think about was Becca. She'd be here soon. Which puppy would she choose? Zoe ran her hand gently down Cookie's back, over and over, as Cookie shook the ball gently to-and-fro, listening to the jingly noises.

"What if she chooses you, Cookie?" Zoe whispered. "I've been trying not to think about it. It was bad enough just thinking about Becca having a dog, and me not being able to have one. But what if it's actually you that she wants to take back with her?" She sighed, and leaned over, resting her cheek against Cookie's wiry fur for a moment. "I suppose at least I'd still get to see you. That's if Becca ever talks to me again, the way I've been this week. I've been awful."

Cookie looked round at her for a moment, her eyes dark and sparkly. She licked Zoe's hand.

"Thank you!" Zoe grinned. "Was that to tell me you don't think I've been awful? I have, though. I was horrible, actually. I just can't tell if it would be worse to never see you again, or to see you belong to someone else! I don't know whether to hope that Becca chooses you or that she doesn't." This time Zoe heaved a massive sigh, so that Cookie turned round and stared at her. "Sorry! Did I shake you up and down?"

"Zoe!" Auntie Jo was calling her. "Becca and her mum and dad are here! They're just getting out of their car. Go and say hello. I'll bring these three in."

"Oh! OK." Zoe gently put Cookie down, and the puppy scampered off after the ball again. She walked slowly through the shelter to the reception area, where Becca and her parents were now talking to Susie, who was on the reception desk.

"You two can chat while we just fill these in," Becca's mum told them, smiling.

Becca couldn't have told her mum how grumpy Zoe had been all week, Zoe realized gratefully. "Hi…" she said to Becca.

"Hi." Becca stared at her, and then

she pulled Zoe over into the corner, as if they were going to look at photos on the wall of the dogs and cats who'd been rehomed recently. "Zoe, is there something going on?" she asked. "Are you mad with me?"

Zoe went red and looked at her feet. "No... I..." She didn't know what to say.

"You are!" Becca cried out. "You've been acting really weird all week! What it it? What have I done?"

Zoe sighed. "Nothing. Nothing at all. I know I've been funny, but it isn't your fault. It's me. I've been jealous ... jealous because you were getting a dog, and I couldn't have one, not ever. We don't have anyone at home to look after a dog, and Kyra hates them anyway. I'm so sorry I've been horrible."

"Oh, Zoe." Becca gave her friend a big hug. "Why didn't you say?" she asked her, stepping back, her eyes round with surprise. "I'd have understood!"

"I suppose I just felt stupid. And mean," Zoe muttered. "And I didn't really want to talk to you about it. You were so excited…"

Becca sighed. "I didn't think about it making you sad," she admitted. "Did I go on and on?"

Zoe gave a very small giggle. "Yes. All the time."

A voice behind them interrupted the awkward moment. It was Becca's dad. "Are you girls ready?" he asked them. "I want to see these wonderful puppies you've been telling me about!"

Becca looked anxiously at Zoe, but Zoe nodded, managing to smile and look almost as though she meant it. "Come on!"

They walked down the passage to the puppies' pen. Zoe spotted Auntie Jo coming back in from the yard, with the puppies in her arms. "There they are," she told Becca's dad, pointing. "They've been playing outside."

The puppies saw them too, and started to wriggle excitedly. Auntie Jo laughed and crouched down, letting them run down the passage towards the visitors.

Cookie dashed ahead, streaking towards Zoe on her tiny little legs. Zoe was desperate to pick her up and cuddle her. But she couldn't. It was Becca's turn.

But Becca wasn't looking at Cookie, Zoe realized. She'd crouched down, and was holding out her arms. Biscuit was running straight up to her, and now he was standing up on his hind legs, his front paws on her arms, giving happy, excited little barks. He licked her cheek and jumped, as though she was the best thing he'd ever seen!

"He remembers me!" Becca cried delightedly. "I've only met him once,

but he really remembers me! Oh, Dad,
do you like him? He's called Biscuit,
he's the most gorgeous of all of them.
Please can he be ours?"

Chapter Eight

Zoe watched, smiling, as Becca hugged Biscuit. He wriggled delightedly in her arms. So it would be a stranger who would be taking Cookie home, she realized sadly. She wouldn't see her gorgeous little puppy grow up into a beautiful dog after all.

Cookie patted her paws hopefully at Zoe's leg, asking to be picked up.

She could tell that Zoe was sad, but Cookie knew that she could make her feel better. When Zoe lifted her up at last, Cookie stood up in her arms, rubbing her whiskery nose against Zoe's cheek. That always made her laugh.

"You're so lovely," Zoe murmured, but she didn't sound much happier.

Cookie watched interestedly as the girl cuddling Biscuit gave him some crunchy treats, and carefully lifted him into a sort of box, like a small pen with a wire front. She shivered a little, burying her nose in Zoe's neck. It reminded her of the box they'd all been shut up in. It felt like a very long time ago now.

Biscuit looked confused, and whined, but the girl fed him some more treats through the wire, and then the man with her picked the box up, and carried him away down the passage to the door.

Cookie gave a little whimper of surprise. They could go away? Biscuit was going with that girl, and the other two people? She didn't understand. If they were allowed out of the shelter, why didn't Zoe take her when she went? Perhaps she would! Perhaps they were all going! Cookie's tail started to flick back and forth with excitement.

"Well, that was good, wasn't it?" Auntie Jo said, sounding really pleased. "And I meant to tell you, Zoe, a really nice-sounding family called me asking about puppies, and they were interested in getting a boy puppy – so that would be you, Choc." She looked down at the puppy in her arms, who'd barked when he heard his name. "Yes, you! They're going to come and see you tomorrow, aren't they, sweetie? So we're getting there."

Zoe nodded. So that would leave just Cookie. And she wouldn't be there for much longer either, Zoe was sure.

"Oh, look, there's your mum and Kyra," Auntie Jo pointed out, and she turned to open the front of the pen, and put Choc back in.

Zoe sighed, and walked towards the pen to put Cookie in too. She'd forgotten that Mum was coming to pick her up early. She wanted them to go and do some shopping – Zoe needed new school shoes. Zoe had tried arguing that Mum could just buy them for her, but Mum had said no.

Cookie twisted in her arms, struggling frantically, and whining. She wasn't going back in the pen – she wanted to stay with Zoe! Someone had already taken Biscuit away. Only Zoe could take her.

"What's the matter?" Zoe gasped, holding the puppy tightly, and backing away from the pen, as that seemed to be what was upsetting her.

"Is Cookie OK?" Mum asked worriedly. She and Kyra had just come into the passage between the pens, and now she was hurrying towards Zoe.

"She got really upset when I was trying to put her back in the pen." Zoe cuddled Cookie close against her shoulder. She could feel the little dog's sides heaving, she was shaking so badly. "Perhaps she's sad about Biscuit going?"

She wrinkled up her brow. "It's OK, Cookie. It's OK," she whispered. But then her eyes filled with tears. "I'm telling her everything's going to be all right, but it isn't," she said miserably, looking between Auntie Jo and Mum. "Biscuit's gone to a new home, and Choc will probably go too, tomorrow, and then it'll be just Cookie left. And someone will choose her really soon, and we'll never see her again."

Auntie Jo frowned. "I wonder if she does know what's happening. Some dogs really do seem to understand, far more than you'd think they could. Maybe that's why she doesn't want to go back into that pen."

"But she has to," Zoe said dismally. "What are we going to do? Do you think she'd be better if we moved her into a different pen?"

Auntie Jo glanced at Mum, and shook her head. "No, to be honest, I think it would just be better if she went back with you."

"But then it would just be harder for her to come back." Zoe blinked, not really understanding what her auntie was saying.

"Or we could keep her?" her mum said, putting an arm round Zoe's shoulders, and gently patting Cookie.

Zoe looked puzzled. "But there's no one to look after her in the daytime."

Her mum glanced at Auntie Jo. "We've been talking about that. I told your auntie I was worried about how much you were falling in love with Cookie. That you were going to be really upset when she went to her new home."

"And I said you were so good with dogs, you really deserved to have one of your own," said Auntie Jo.

"So we've come up with a plan," said her mum.

"I'm going to have her here at work with me in the day, Zoe," Auntie Jo explained. "She can have a basket under my desk, and I'll take her for a walk at lunchtime."

"And Kyra?" said Zoe, flashing her sister a look.

"I don't feel scared of Cookie," said Kyra. "She's a little sweetheart. Mum told me how much you'd bonded with Cookie – it was actually my idea we should have her. That's why I wanted to meet her last week."

"Really?" Zoe stared round at them all, her eyes like saucers. "You mean it? We can have Cookie? So – so we could take her home now?" Zoe whispered, hardly daring to hope that they'd say yes.

Auntie Jo smiled. "Well, she obviously doesn't want to go back in that pen. I can stay here and make a big fuss of poor old Choc, so he doesn't mind being on his own. And you can borrow some food bowls and things, until you can get your own."

Zoe nodded, thinking how much pocket money she had saved up, and how she was going to spend all of it at the pet shop on the little puppy. Cookie was going to have the nicest things she could find.

"You're coming home with us," she

whispered to Cookie. "You really are."

Cookie nudged Zoe's cheek with her damp black nose, and looked hopefully at the door.

"Look at them! They're having such a good time," Zoe said, laughing at the two little brown-and-white dogs – Biscuit and Cookie. Who would have thought it? They were standing at the bottom of a huge tree, right at the end of their extending leads. And they were both jumping up and down, barking themselves silly.

"I wonder if Choc likes chasing squirrels too?" Becca said thoughtfully. "Maybe we'll see him in the park one of these days."

Zoe nodded. "I bet he does. And I bet he never catches them either."

The squirrel was sitting high up in the tree now, looking down at the two dogs in disgust. They hadn't come anywhere near getting him, and he clearly wasn't very bothered. He almost looked like he was yawning.

Eventually, Cookie and Biscuit gave up on the squirrel and wandered back to Zoe and Becca.

"Cookie's catching up on him," Becca commented. "She's nearly as big as he is now. She might even end up being bigger!"

"Maybe," Zoe agreed. "They probably won't finish growing until they're about nine months. Perhaps even a year. They're four months old now, so they've got five months more growing to do, at least. You're going to be a huge dog one day, aren't you?" she told Cookie affectionately, crouching down and ruffling her ears and stroking her back.

Becca giggled. Cookie might get bigger one day, but she and Biscuit were still tiny at the moment. Not that they seemed to think they were little at all. They strutted through the park as though they thought they were the most important dogs there.

"They wouldn't fit in that box now," Zoe said suddenly, looking up at Becca.

Becca shook her head. "I still don't know how someone could have left them like that. But I'm just glad it was you and your Auntie Jo that found them."

Zoe nodded, scratching Cookie under the chin, so that she closed her eyes blissfully, and her tail thumped on the ground.

"I know. Me too."